DAKOTA CRUMB

TINY TREASURE HUNTER

Jamie Michalak *illustrated by* Kelly Murphy

CANDLEWICK PRESS

IN THE GREAT, BIG CITY,
in the great, big museum,
a clock tick-tocks past midnight.

Doors are locked.
Guards keep watch.
All is still, until . . .

a small figure creeps out of the shadows!

Hundreds of eyes follow tiny paws
silently scurrying down the Great Hall.
Who is this mouse of mystery?

It's Dakota Crumb,

tiny treasure hunter,
carrying a sack and a treasure map!

For endless nights, Dakota has searched
for a famous priceless treasure.
It's hidden in an unknown place
called the Deepest, Darkest Cave—
X marks the spot.

But a dangerous journey still lies ahead.

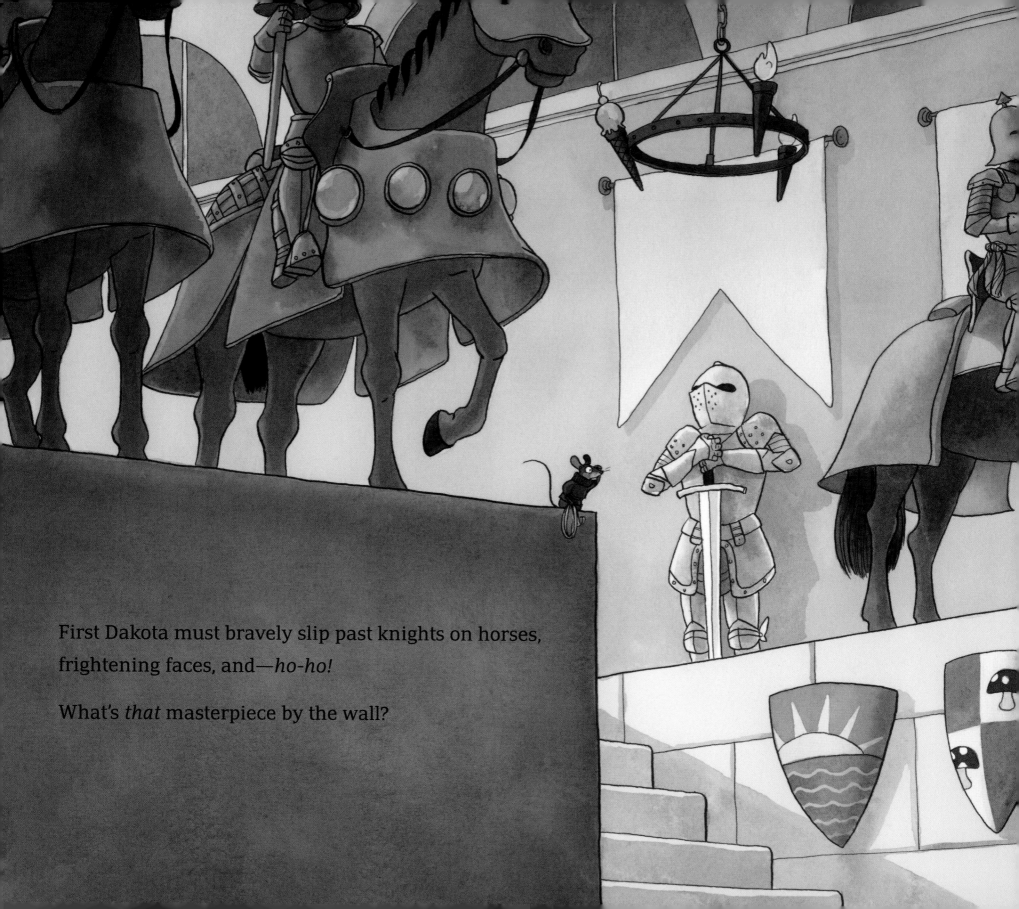

First Dakota must bravely slip past knights on horses, frightening faces, and—*ho-ho!*

What's *that* masterpiece by the wall?

Guest Book

DOOR
Had such a great visit! -Gort, IRE
THIS IS A BEAUTIFUL MUSEUM. THANK YOU! - FIONA
erfect! -Anna
have lots of fun.

Swing.

Swoop.

Swipe!

A beautiful painting.

Into Dakota's sack it goes!

But it's not the famous treasure.
Dakota studies her map and searches on . . .

to the moonlit room.
Dakota shivers as frozen giants loom above,
staring, glaring, and—*aha!*
A long-lost statue lurks nearby.
Creep.
Crawl . . .

Whoosh!
   WHOA!

Too slow.
Dakota escapes by a whisker.

Heave-ho! Into Dakota's sack it goes!

Tick-tock goes the clock.

But where's the treasure?

Dakota checks her map and travels on . . .

to the land of Egypt.

Legend has it that an old pirate mouse
hid the famous Purple Jewel of Egypt here—

in the Deepest, Darkest Cave.

Dakota spies
mummies,
an ancient temple,
and a scary creature guarding it:

A GIANT . . .

EVIL-EYED . . .

MOUSE-EATING . . .

CAT!

Dakota freezes in fear.

The cat is big. Dakota is small.

But small can be brave.

Scurry.

Hurry!

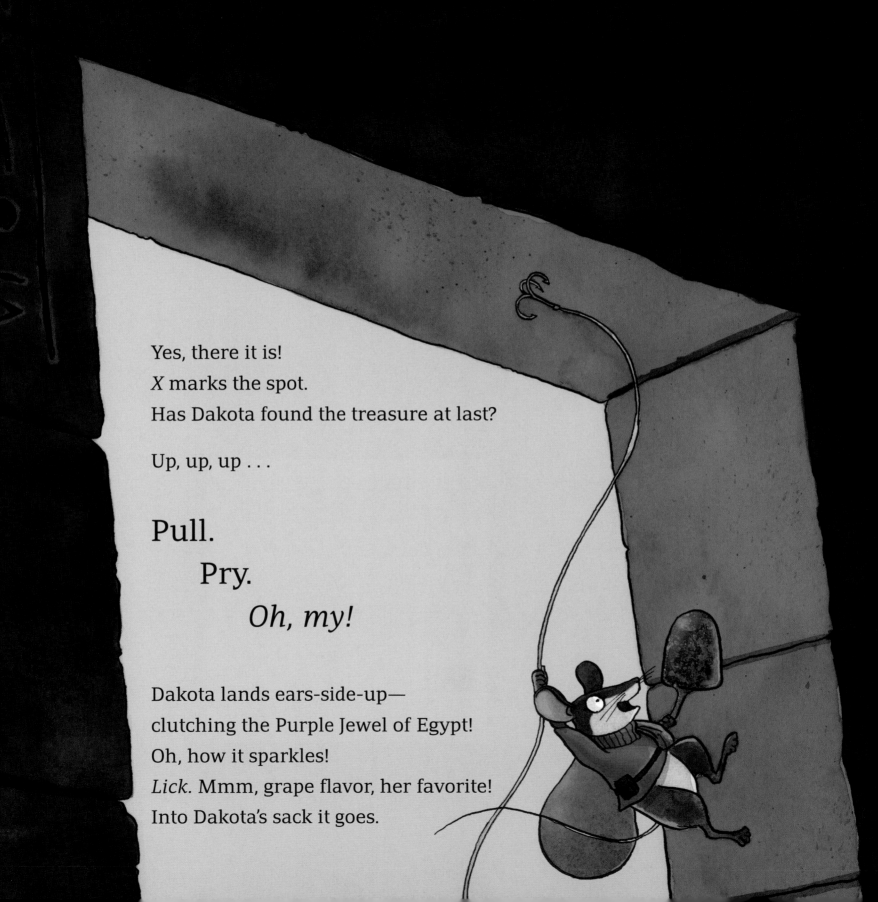

Yes, there it is!
X marks the spot.
Has Dakota found the treasure at last?

Up, up, up . . .

Pull.
     Pry.
          Oh, my!

Dakota lands ears-side-up—
clutching the Purple Jewel of Egypt!
Oh, how it sparkles!
Lick. Mmm, grape flavor, her favorite!
Into Dakota's sack it goes.

Silently scurrying back down the Great Hall,
carrying a full sack,
Dakota Crumb, tiny treasure hunter, heads home.
Just in time, too. The sun is rising.

WELCOME!

In the great, big city,
under the great, big museum,
a line of visitors waits by a teeny-tiny door.
Inside they'll find . . .

a familiar-looking mouse, twinkly-eyed from midnight adventures.

"Welcome to my Mousehole Museum!" Miss Crumb says with a wink.

Want to go on another treasure hunt?
Explore the inside and outside of the
great, big museum again using
Dakota Crumb's list.

cheese

cherries

ketchup packet

thread

pop top

jelly beans

crayon

whistle

button pin

popcorn

candy

paper crane

walnut shell

doll shoe

letter

apple core

top

paddle ball toy

birthday hat

matchstick

yo-yo

needle

thumb tack

Dakota didn't find these things, but maybe you can!

oat cereal

flowers

mushroom

bird in nest

candy corn

ice cream cone

feather

seashell

domino

peanut

lipstick

diamond

acorn

puzzle piece

tooth

paw print

die

lollipop

banana

leaf

candy cane

hummingbird

To Julie, small and brave
JM

For Fiona and Finnegan,
two very mischievous mice
KM

First edition 2021

Library of Congress Catalog Card Number pending
ISBN 978-1-5362-0394-3

21 22 23 24 25 26 CCP 10 9 8 7 6 5 4 3 2 1

Printed in Shenzhen, Guangdong, China

This book was typeset in Adamant.
The illustrations were done in pen and ink, colored digitally.

Candlewick Press
99 Dover Street
Somerville, Massachusetts 02144

www.candlewick.com